I had the silliest dream last night about two monkeys swinging in a tree! Jumpy and Sunny were on their way to jungle school.

Jumpy the monkey was loud and jumped all around. But when he got to jungle school, he used his breathing to calm himself down.

Mindful Me, Happy Me™

Stay Cool at School

By Lori Lite

Illustrated by Richard Watson

Scholastic Inc.

The publisher thanks author Lori Lite for her creative contributions to the series title *Mindful Me, Happy Me™*.

ISBN 978-1-338-24471-7

10 9 8 7 6 5 4 3 2 1   18 19 20 21 22

Printed in the U.S.A.   40
First printing 2018

Book design by Lizzy Yoder

Jumpy put his hands on his belly and breathed in deeply. He felt his belly move up and down. He felt calm breathing in 1, 2, 3 and out 1, 2, 3.

Sunny the monkey liked to laugh, run, and play. But when she needed to be calm, she used her quiet words to relax. Sunny said to herself, "I am calm, I am calm, I am calm."

Sometimes I feel worried about following the rules at school, knowing when to be quiet, and how to be still. Maybe Jumpy and Sunny can show me how to calm down when I need to.

"Good morning!" Mom tells me to rise and shine. But I feel like a sleepyhead.

I wonder what Jumpy the monkey would do when he feels tired or worries about getting ready for jungle school.

Jumpy stretches his body and takes in a big breath. He lets the air out of his mouth with an "ahhhh." This helps him wake up so his day can begin.

Mom tells me to hurry up, get dressed, and find my backpack for school. I look around, but my backpack is nowhere to be found. I feel frustrated when I can't find my backpack.

I wonder what Sunny would do when she feels frustrated getting ready for jungle school.

Sunny takes in a deep breath and tells herself, "I am calm, I am calm, I am calm."

The school bus driver tells me to sit down. But someone is sitting in my favorite seat. "Uh-oh." I feel nervous about sitting in a different seat.

I wonder what Jumpy would do when he feels nervous on his way to jungle school.

Jumpy takes in a deep breath and lets the air out through his nose. He feels calm breathing in 1, 2, 3 and out 1, 2, 3.

My teacher tells me to settle down and use
my inside, quiet voice. But I feel excited, and I want to use my
outside voice to talk to my friends.

I wonder what Sunny would do when she feels too excited at jungle school.

Sunny takes in a deep breath and tells herself, "I am calm, I am calm, I am calm."

My teacher says it is time to play ball outside, to be mindful, and to share. But I feel angry when I can't keep the ball for myself. "It's mine!" is what I want to say.

I wonder what Jumpy would do when he feels angry at jungle school.

Jumpy takes in a deep breath and lets the air out through his nose. He feels calm breathing in 1, 2, 3 and out 1, 2, 3.

At lunchtime I wait in line for mac and cheese. No pushing, no shoving, and always say please. But I feel impatient and do not want to wait my turn.

I wonder what Sunny would do when she feels impatient at jungle school.

Sunny takes in a deep breath and tells herself, "I am calm, I am calm, I am calm."

Arts and crafts class is so much fun. But I spilled my paint when I painted the sun. "Oh no!" I feel embarrassed when I see that I spilled.

I wonder what Jumpy would do when he feels embarrassed at jungle school.

Jumpy takes in a deep breath and lets the air out through his nose. He feels calm breathing in 1, 2, 3 and out 1, 2, 3.

"Yay!" The school bell rings, and it's time to go home.

After supper, Mom tells me it is time to take a bath, brush my teeth, and get into bed.

But I don't feel like a sleepyhead.

I feel wide awake, and I want to run and jump until it's late. I wonder what Jumpy and Sunny would do when their day is done after jungle school.

Sunny takes in a deep breath and tells herself, "I am calm, I am calm, I am calm." And Jumpy breathes in 1, 2, 3 and out 1, 2, 3.

"Hooray for me!" I was mindful at school and had a great day.
Now I know when to calm down and when it is okay to play.
Thanks to Jumpy and Sunny, I know just what to do!

I tell myself, "I am calm, I am calm, I am calm." And I breathe in
1, 2, 3 and out 1, 2, 3.

About This Book:

Stay Cool at School addresses the range of emotions children experience throughout their day. Jumpy and Sunny help children identify their big emotions and use tools to cope. With practice, children become empowered to use their own set of coping skills.

Parents can integrate this story and its techniques into their family's everyday life and bedtime routine. Teachers can use this book at school to create emotional awareness and ease transitions.

Helpful Tips:

* Help children identify and manage their feelings in the classroom and at home by labeling their feelings with words.

* Let children know it is okay to express their feelings. Even teachers, moms, and dads at times feel worried, frustrated, nervous, excited, angry, impatient, and embarrassed.

* Pause during real-life moments and demonstrate how you as an adult or teacher use the techniques.

* Instead of telling children to "calm down," show them *how* by using the techniques in this story. Encourage them to breathe in 1,2,3 and out 1,2,3.

* Reference Jumpy and Sunny when talking about how to calm down. "What does Jumpy do when he feels nervous?" "What does Sunny do when she is embarrassed?" Or, "Let's see how we feel if we do our Jumpy breathing." "Let's see how we can settle down when we use our quiet words like Sunny."

* Practice these self-soothing techniques with children during calm moments.

Managing big feelings in a healthy way is something we can all learn. With repetition, these self-soothing techniques can become a go-to tool in your child's emotional backpack.